THE BERRY BASKET

Three African Tales
Retold by Dinah M. Mbanze
With illustrations by Niki Daly

Kwela
BOOKS

Edited by Jo Bleeker
Cover and design concept by The Inkman
Set in Bodoni 16 on 20 pt
Printed and bound by NBD
Drukkery Street, Goodwood, Western Cape

First edition, first printing 1999

ISBN 0-7957-0100-4

❡ INDEX ❡

THE THREE SISTERS

Once upon a time there was a Giant Man-Eater who lived in a far-away forest surrounded by mountains and rivers.

His name was Izimuzimu and he was extremely ugly. Izimuzimu liked to kill humans and eat their flesh.

Near the edge of the forest lived a family – a father, a mother and their three daughters.

One day the daughters asked for permission to go to the nearby mountain to pick umnombela – sweet berries.

"Please, please, may we go?" they begged.

"Why do you want to go and collect berries?" their mother asked.

"I have heard that the berries are as sweet as honey," the eldest sister said.

"We have always wanted to taste the sweet berries," the second sister said. "They are even sweeter than honey, I hear."

"Please, please, may we go?" the little sister begged. She jumped up and down with excitement.

"Will you be careful?" their father asked. "Izimuzimu, the Giant Man-Eater, lives in the forest," he warned them.

"Yes, yes. We will be very careful," they promised.

"Then you may go," said their mother. "But remember, you must to be home before dark."

Now the oldest sister did not want the youngest sister to go with them, as she did not want to look after her.

"Little sister, you may not come with us," the oldest sister said. "You have to stay at home."

The youngest sister began to cry. She cried and cried. "Please! Please, let me go with you!" she cried.

"Oh, alright then! But you have to carry your own basket."

Each sister took her own berry basket and they left for the mountain. They walked and they walked for a long time.

At last they reached the mountain where the sweet berries grew. Each went in a different direction as they started to fill their baskets.

Late that afternoon when their baskets were brimming over with berries, they called to each other, because they had promised to be home before dark.

When they gathered together, they
discovered that the youngest sister had
picked only green berries. The oldest
sister became very cross and she
began to scold the youngest sister.
The little sister pleaded with her older
sisters to help her pick ripe berries.

8

When they refused to help, she began to cry bitterly. "Please, please come and help me pick some ripe berries!" she begged.

At first her sisters did not want to help her, but she was crying so much that they agreed to help her.

By the time they had filled her basket with ripe berries, it was very late and almost dark. They decided to hurry back home.

The three sisters had travelled only a short distance when the sun went down behind the mountain. Soon it was dark. Although they walked very fast, they seemed to stand still. And the faster they walked, the darker it became. Soon it was too dark to walk. The sisters knew they would not reach their home that night.

They became frightened. The oldest
sister did not know what to do.
Suddenly she saw a fire blazing in the
distance.

"Let's go to the fire and ask the
people for a place to sleep," she said.
She did not know it was the home of
Izimuzimu, the Giant Man-Eater of
the forest.

When they arrived at the home
where the fire was, the sisters knocked
on the door.

"Siyakhuleka! Kwabasekhaya! –
Please open for us! Please let us sleep
with you!" they cried.

An ugly old woman came out and
greeted them.

"I don't know where I'm going to
hide you. My husband is a giant who
eats human flesh. He will kill you if he
finds you here!" she scolded.

But because she felt sorry for the sisters, the old woman prepared a place for them to sleep.

As she had no blankets, she handed them some old torn clothes and told them to hide.

The house was terribly dirty and there were nasty insects – bedbugs, lice and fleas. The three sisters could not sleep because the insects crawled onto their bodies.

The bedbugs bit them; the lice bit them, and the fleas jumped all over them until their skins burned. After a while the ugly Giant Man-Eater, Izimuzimu, arrived home.

He sniffed the air as he entered and roared, "I can smell inyama-nyama yami – pieces of tasty meat!"

Then the Giant Man-Eater began looking around for human flesh. He kept feeling around in the darkness and asking, "Are you asleep? Are you asleep?"

Finally the sisters answered, "No! No! We are not sleeping because the bedbugs are biting us!"

As soon he heard them, Izimuzimu knew they were hiding in the back-room.

He threw some more dirty, torn clothes to them and told them to wear the clothes so that they could sleep well. Then he, too, went to sleep.

After some time Izimuzimu returned to the back-room and again asked, "Hey! Are you still asleep?"

The two older sisters were fast asleep. But the youngest sister was hard at work – catching bedbugs, lice and fleas and putting them into six claypots that she had found in the room.

"No! No! We are being bitten by the bedbugs!" she replied.

Izimuzimu became very angry and said to her, "Hey! You are a trouble-maker!"

Then he gave her some more torn clothes and told her to go to sleep.

Three times he asked her, "Are you asleep?" and three times she gave him the same answer. All the while she was filling the claypots with insects and looking for something to help her and her sisters escape from Izimuzimu.

She searched and searched in the room. At last she found three magic eggs and three wooden pounding blocks.

First she took the wooden pounding blocks and dressed them like girls with the torn clothing. Then she put them down on the floor to look like three sleeping girls.

15

The youngest sister then woke up the two older sisters. "Come! Come! Let us run away! Izimuzimu is coming to kill us!" she whispered.

Quickly, they followed her out of the house.

After some time Izimuzimu woke up and asked the same question again, "Hey! Are you still asleep?"

There was no answer.

Three times he asked the same question. When there was no answer, he became furious and went into the room to kill the sisters and eat them.

He took his axe in both hands and
began to chop the first girl – but the
axe bounced off the wooden pounding
block and hurt his leg.

Izimuzimu cried out to his wife for
help. She woke up and put a bandage
on his sore leg.

He was enraged because the sisters
had made a fool of him.

He rushed outside and sniffed the air.
When he caught their scent, he gave
chase, limping on his sore leg.

The sisters ran and ran. They grew
tired but they kept on running. As
Izimuzimu came near them, the little
sister threw down the first claypot.

Izimuzimu picked up the claypot and cracked it open with his axe. Then he sat and ate the insects one by one until the claypot was empty. That done, he jumped up and pursued the sisters again.

Two, three, four, five, six times the youngest sister threw down a claypot. And every time Izimuzimu sat down and ate the insects one by one.

Every time he sang the same song: *"Inyamanyama yami! To-dongela! To-dongela – My tasty pieces of meat! I'll eat them! I'll eat them!"*

The sisters kept running as fast as they could, but Izimuzimu always managed catch up with them. When the six clay-pots had all been thrown down, the little sister decided to use the magic eggs.

When Izimuzimu came near them again, she threw down the first magic egg. Magically, the egg grew into a hill.

It was the biggest hill Izimuzimu had ever seen. He stood thinking for a while. Then he returned to his house where he put down his axe and picked up a spade.

He ran back, removed the hill with his
spade and continued to chase the girls.
When he came near them, raising a
cloud of dust, the little sister again
threw down a magic egg.

The magic egg changed into a tree.

While the little sister sang a song to
the tree, the three sisters climbed into
its branches.

*"Sihlahla, sihlahla, khulela phezulu.
Sihlahla, sihlahla, khulela phezulu –*
Tree, tree, grow taller and taller," she
sang.

The tree grew taller and taller and
bigger and bigger.

The ugly Izimuzimu stood under the
tree and said, "Tree, become smaller!"

But the youngest sister kept on
singing to the tree to grow taller and
bigger.

Filled with rage, Izimuzimu went
back home to fetch his axe to chop
down the tree.

As soon as he was gone, the youngest
sister sang to the tree: *"Tree, tree,
please become a small tree again!"*

The tree became smaller and smaller. So they climbed out of the tree and ran away.

They had only one magic egg left, but they were now much closer to their home.

The three sisters were exhausted, but they kept up the pace. After a while they saw that the ugly Izimuzimu was again only a little way behind them – and getting nearer and nearer!

The youngest sister was terrified. She began to cry and plead with the egg. "Please, Magic Egg, save our lives!" she cried as she threw down the last egg.

Her tears fell onto the magic egg as she cried.

Then a wonderful thing happened –
the tears which rolled from her eyes
onto the magic egg became a river!

The youngest sister clapped her
hands when she saw the magic egg
had made a wide river from her tears.

The river grew so wide that the water
separated the sisters from the angry
flesh-eating giant. Izimuzimu was on
one side of the river and the sisters
were safely on the other side.

The ugly human flesh-eating giant sat down on the bank of the river and wailed because he could not catch the three sisters. His tears flowed into the river, making it grow even wider and wider.

On the opposite bank, the three sisters washed their tired feet in the rushing water.

Then they walked slowly home and never again returned to pick the sweet, sweet berries that grow on the mountain, near the forest, where Izimuzimu still lives.

THE TALKATIVE WIFE

Long ago a man and his wife lived near a forest and a river. The man was a hunter and a fisherman. In the morning the man went to the forest to catch animals. In the afternoon he went fishing in the river. The man was very smart – he caught many animals and lots of fish. So there was always enough food to eat.

But the man was very unhappy. He had a lot of trouble with his wife. Each time he brought home some animals or some fish, his wife told everyone about it.

All the people, young and old, always
knew what the man had caught in the
forest and in the river.

The wife did not like to work hard.
Every day, as soon as her husband had
left for the forest, she went to visit a
neighbour. She told the neighbour
everything about her husband's hunting
and fishing. When the hard-working man
came home at night, the neighbours
knew what he had caught and he always
had to gove them some of the catch.

The man thought and thought
about his wife who talked too much.
He decided to teach her a lesson.
But he did not know how to make the
neighbours stop believing his wife's
many stories.

One day the man caught an animal.

When he went to the river, he saw
that he had caught a fish too. He sat
down and thought about the animal
and the fish. Then he made a plan.
He hooked the animal onto the fishing
rod and took the fish to the forest.

He put the fish into the snare with
which he had caught the animal.

The next day he asked his wife to go
to the forest with him. She was only
too happy to go.

When they came to the snare in the
forest, they found a fish caught in it.
The wife was very surprised to find
a fish in the forest. She was very
excited. She had great news to tell the
neighbours when they returned home!

"Neighbour, neighbour! Do you know what I saw?" the wife cried.

"No, what did you see?" the neighbour asked.

"I saw a most wonderful thing!" she answered. "My husband caught a fish in a snare in the forest!"

"Ee! Ee! That cannot be!" the neighbour said. "Your husband cannot catch a fish in a snare!"

"It is true!" she cried.

The next day the husband asked his wife to go to the river with him. She was only too happy to go!

When they came to the river, what did they see?

There was an animal on the fishing rod!

"Ee! Ee! This is wonderful!" exclaimed the wife. She was very, very excited. What great news – an animal on the fishing rod and a fish in a snare!

As soon as they got home, she knocked on the neighbour's door. Her husband watched to see what would happen.

When the neighbour opened the door, she saw the wife had a story to tell. "Neighbour, neighbour, do you know what I saw?" she cried.

"No, what did you see?" the neighbour asked.

"I saw another wonderful thing," she answered. "My husband caught an animal in the river with his fishing rod!"

"Ee! Ee! That cannot be true!" the neighbour said.

"It is true! It is true!" the wife cried.

But the neighbour laughed at her. And when the neighbour told the other neighbours, they said, "You tell us a thing that cannot be true. You are a liar!"

So the neighbours gave her a new name: "Mother Lie".

Whenever she told her stories they all laughed at her and sang, *"Mother Lie, Mother Lie!"*

From that day on, the husband was a truly happy man because no one believed anything his wife said – ever again!

THE FRIENDLY MONSTER

Once upon a time there was an old king who had many, many wives. He married all the young girls of the village. They all became his queens. But the young queens were not happy, because the king kept them in his palace like captives.

The king was a bad ruler. Whenever
he wanted something from someone,
he just took it. He took the largest
oxen, the biggest goats, the fattest
roosters, and the hens which lay the
most eggs. The people in the village,
the servants in the palace, and the
soldiers did not like the king.

But they were afraid of him.

One day the king saw another beautiful young girl who he wanted to marry. But she was in love with a young herd-boy.

The king sent his soldiers to capture the young herd-boy. He ordered them to kill him and throw him into the dam.

In the dam there was a monster who lived from eating fish. Every day after he had eaten fish, he came to the surface of the water and roared like a lion. Then he disappeared into the water again and slept until the next day.

All the people in the village were afraid of the monster.

All the people in the village were afraid of the monster. "If you go near the dam, the Big Monster will eat you!" the mothers warned their children.

The women in the village were also afraid of the monster. "If you draw water from the dam, the Big Monster will eat you!" one woman said to another woman.

From then on the women did not go near the dam.

The men in the village were afraid of the monster too. "Do not let your cattle drink water from the dam!" one man said to another man.

"The Big Monster will eat you!" that man said to another man. "The Big Monster will also eat your cattle!"

From that day on, the men did not go near the dam.

But the Big Monster was not really a bad monster – he did not eat humans, he only ate fish.

When the soldiers threw the body of the young herd-boy into the dam, the monster caught it. He took the herd-boy and blew into his face.

That woke him up. From then on the herd-
boy lived with the monster in the dam.

The young girl was heart-broken when she
heard that her lover had been killed by the
king's soldiers.

But that night the young girl had a
dream. She dreamt she was drawing water
from the dam when the Big Monster
appeared. She wanted to run away, but
her legs felt too heavy for her to move.

"Do not be afraid, young girl," the monster said to her.

The monster did not sound like a bad monster. Indeed, when she looked at the monster, she saw a wonderful thing happen – the face of the monster became the face of her lover.

Overjoyed, she wanted to jump into the dam. But the monster said, "No! There is something you have to do for the people of the village."

"What must I do, Big Monster-With-The-Face-Of-My-Lover?" she asked.

"Before the king marries you to-morrow, you must run away!"

"Where must I run to, Big Monster?" she asked.

"Run into the dam, my love!" he said.

When the young girl heard the monster calling her "my love", she was not afraid of him any more.

The next day the king ordered the soldiers to call all the people to the palace.

"Quick! Quick! Come to the palace. The king is to be married!" the soldiers shouted as they walked through the village.

But an odd thing happened:

The people could not walk quickly.

When they tried to walk, their feet
only moved in short, little steps.

The soldiers could not walk properly
either. When the king called them,
they went slowly to the palace – taking
short, little steps.

The king became angry and shouted,
"Move your feet! Move your feet!"

When the young girl saw how slowly everyone moved, she remembered her dream and began running towards the dam. Her feet moved like the wind!

The king shouted furiously, "Catch her!"

But his soldiers were too slow. So the king ran after the girl himself.

But she was too quick. When she came to the dam, she jumped right in!

The king jumped into the dam after her.

Ee! Ee! The Big Monster caught the king and swallowed him.

Then the monster came out of the water and roared like a lion!

Another odd thing happened:

The soldiers and the servants and the people could suddenly move again! They were so pleased that the king had been swallowed by the monster that they began to dance and sing.

A wonderful thing then happened:
The young girl and the herd-boy came
out of the dam.

Everyone was so happy to see them that
they made the herd-boy and the young
girl the new king and queen of the village.

And what did the new queen do?

She opened the doors of the palace and
let all the young girls go home.

And what did the new king do?

He saw to it that the monster had enough fish to eat.

And what did the Big Monster do?

He came out of the water and roared like a lion!

And what did the people in the village do?

The people in the village just went on with their work because they were no longer afraid of the Big Monster in the dam!

Something about the Author and Illustrator

DINAH M. MBANZE
taught at a farm school in the district of Bronkhorstspruit in
Gauteng until 1998, when, after thirty years, she was retrenched
because she lacked formal teaching qualifications. At the
suggestion of Jo Bleeker of Tweefontein farm where Dinah lives,
she then started to write down the tales she had heard as a child.
With the assistence of Jo Bleeker the stories were later prepared
and presented for publication.

NIKI DALY
is an international award-winning illustrator and writer of children's picture books. In 1995 *All the Magic in the World* earned
him an IBBY Honours Award for Illustration, and the New York
Times Literary Supplement selected his *Why the Sun and Moon
Live in the Sky* as one of the ten best illustrated books published
in the USA that year. In 1996 the same book won the Anne Izard
Story Teller's Choice Award, and in 1998 *Bravo, Zan Angelo*
received the Parent's Choice Award for Illustration. Niki lives in
Cape Town in the Western Cape.